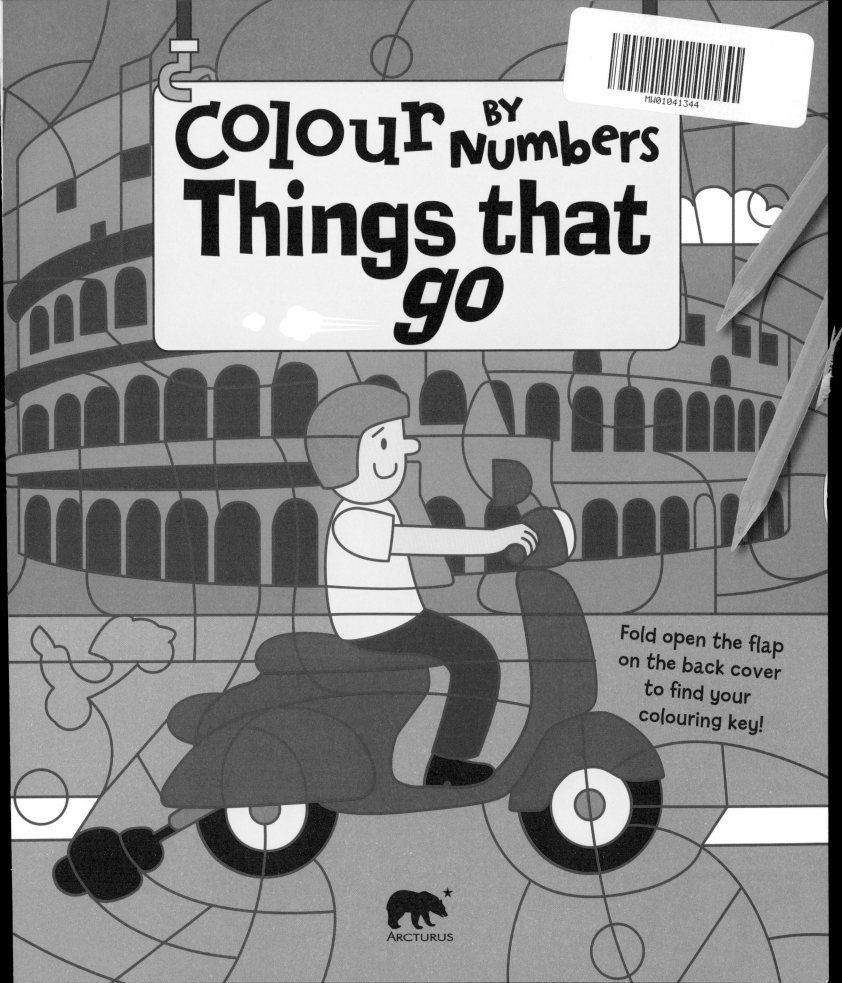

Colour BY Numbers
Things that go

Fold open the flap on the back cover to find your colouring key!

ARCTURUS

ARCTURUS

This edition published in 2017 by Arcturus Publishing Limited
26/27 Bickels Yard, 151–153 Bermondsey Street,
London SE1 3HA

ISBN: 978-1-78428-684-2
CH005530NT
Supplier 26, Date 0817, Print run 6206

Illustrations by Collaborate

Printed in China

Let's colour!

Fold out the flap on the cover of this book and use it as a guide to complete the pictures. From helicopters to hang gliders, and sports cars to speedboats, there's so much to colour. Watch out for the hidden pictures, too – they're not all they seem!

Would you like to fly in our beautiful balloon?

Look at the plane taking off!

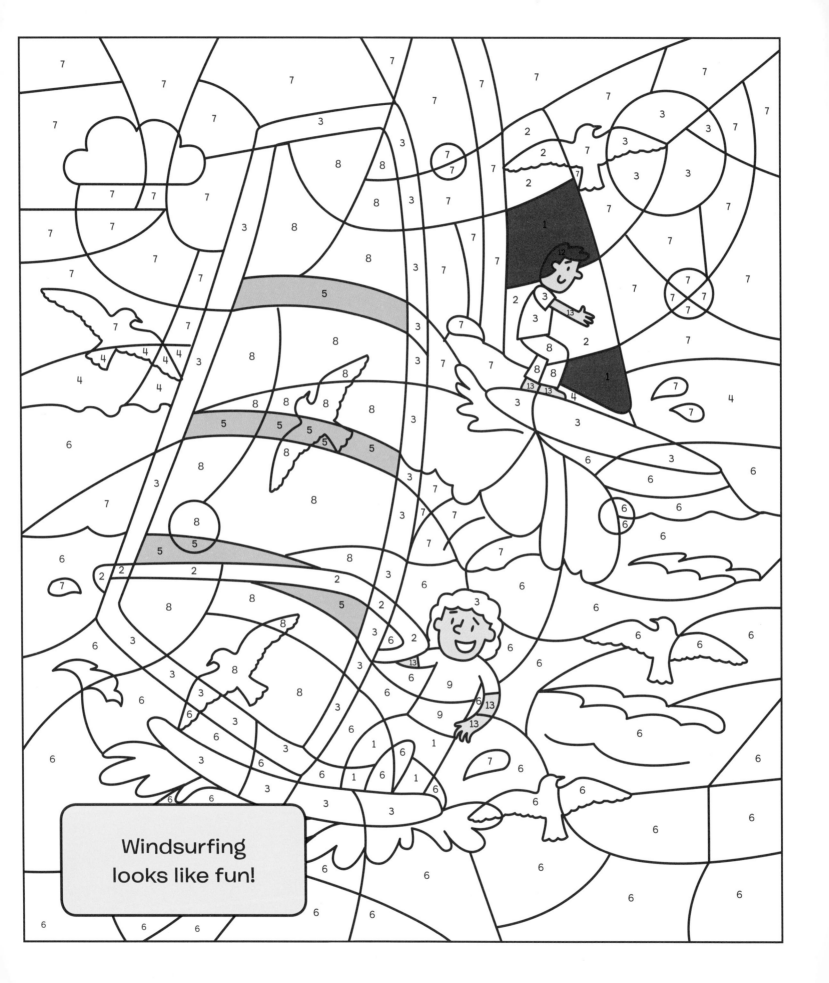

Windsurfing looks like fun!

This man is very brave!

What a monster truck!

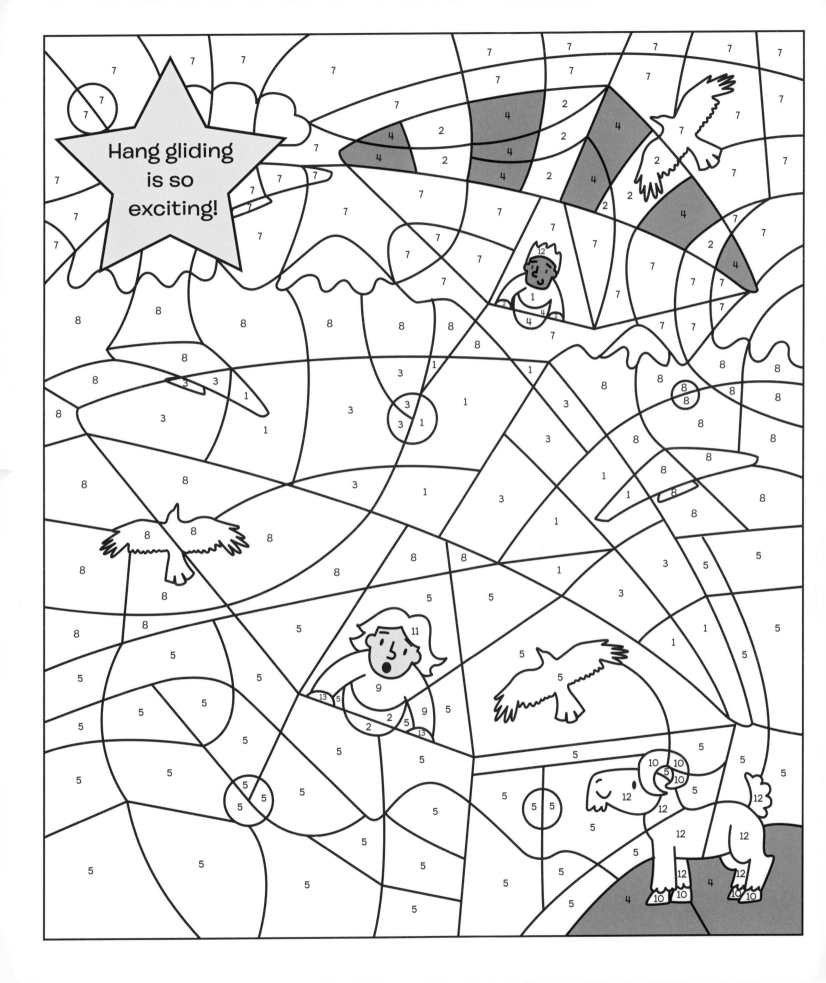

Hang gliding is so exciting!

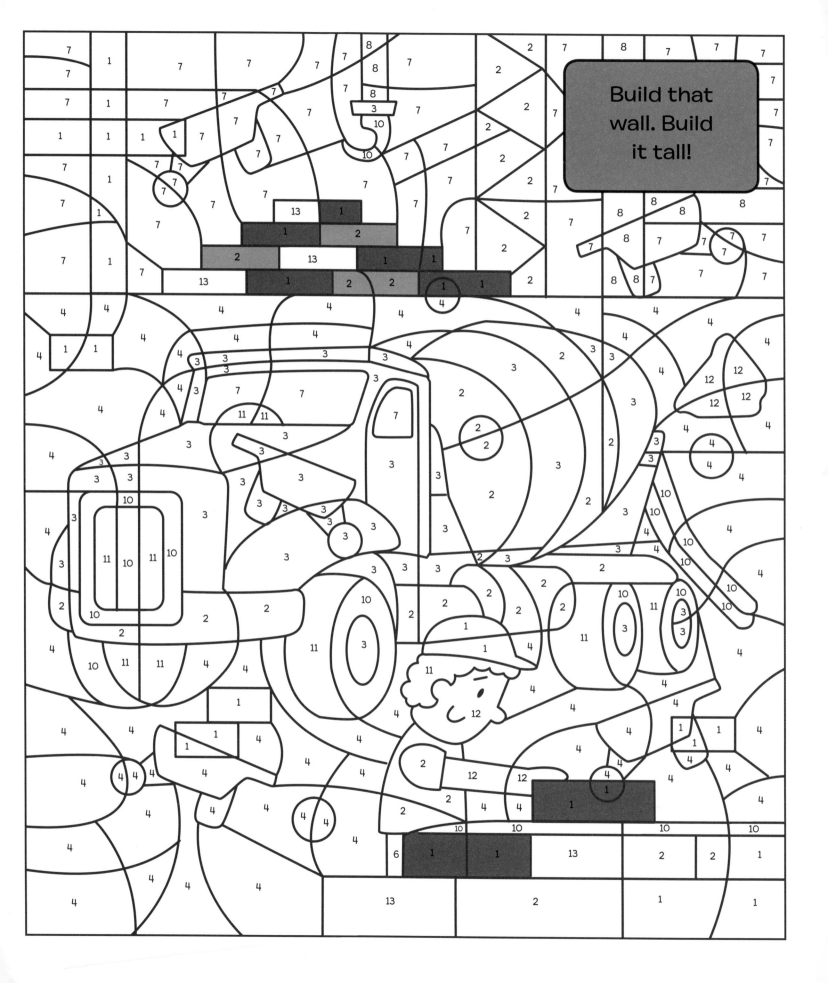

Build that wall. Build it tall!

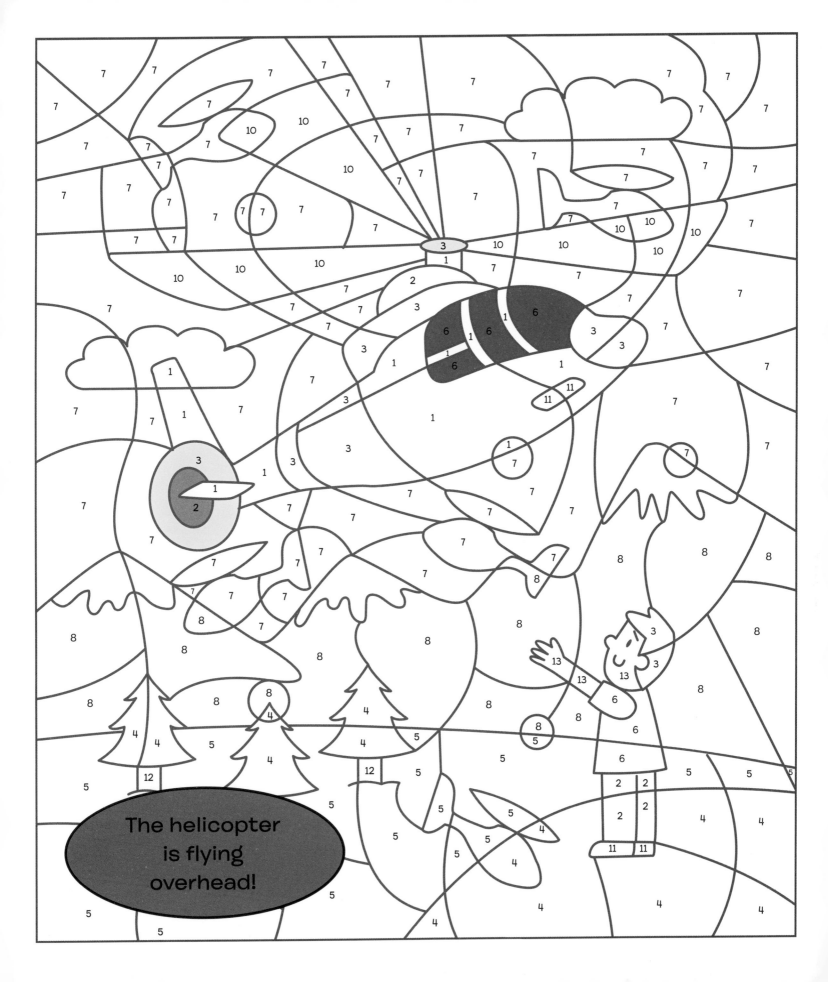

What noise does an ambulance make?

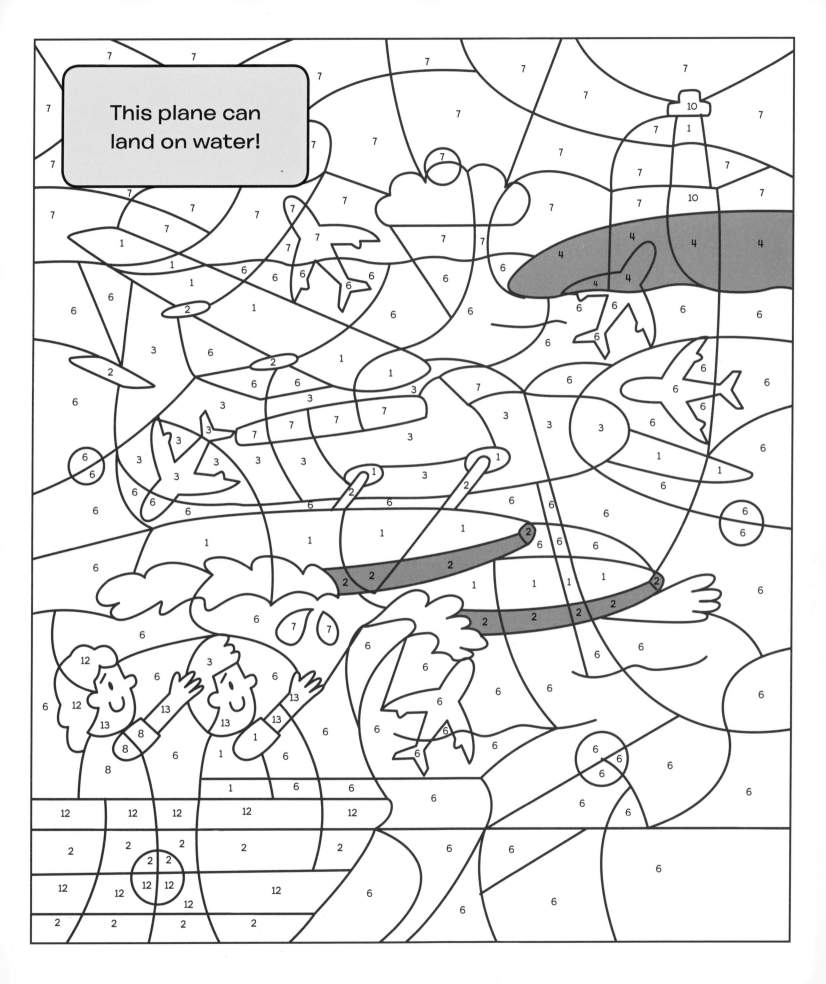

This plane can land on water!

This digger has a backhoe.

It's a race to the finish!

These huskies are cute!

This sailor is heading out to sea.

This man is
on holiday
in Rome!

Fly with me to the stars!

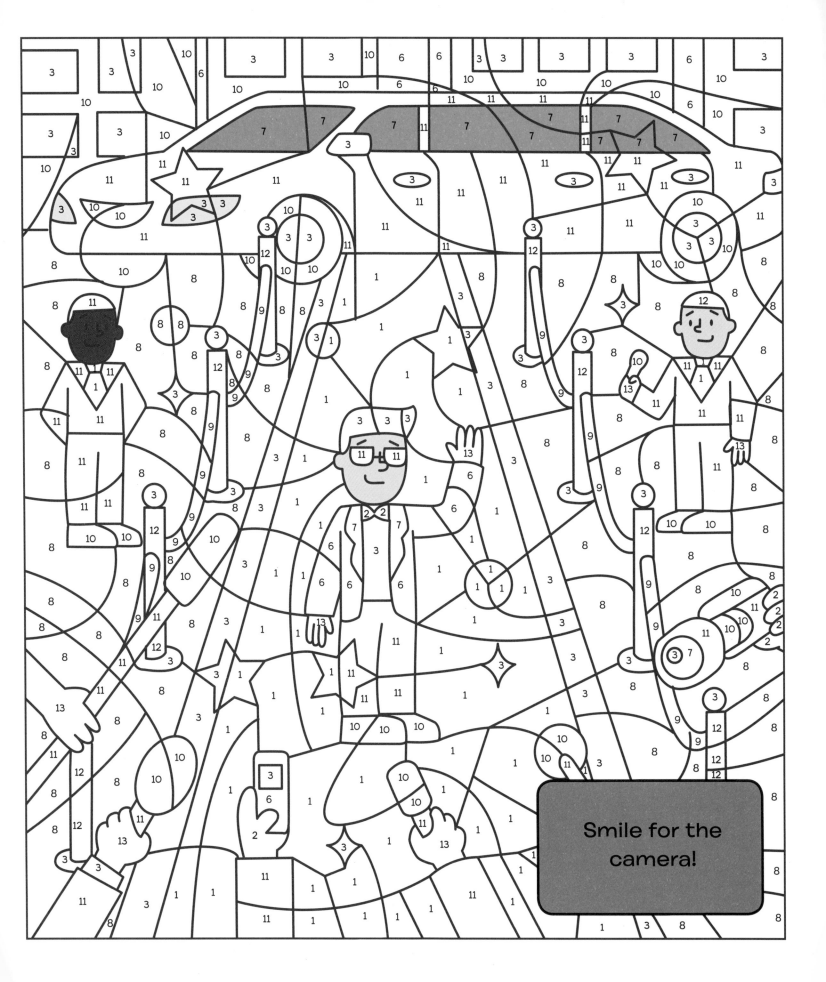

Smile for the camera!

This car is the fastest one in the world!

This little car is a tuk-tuk.

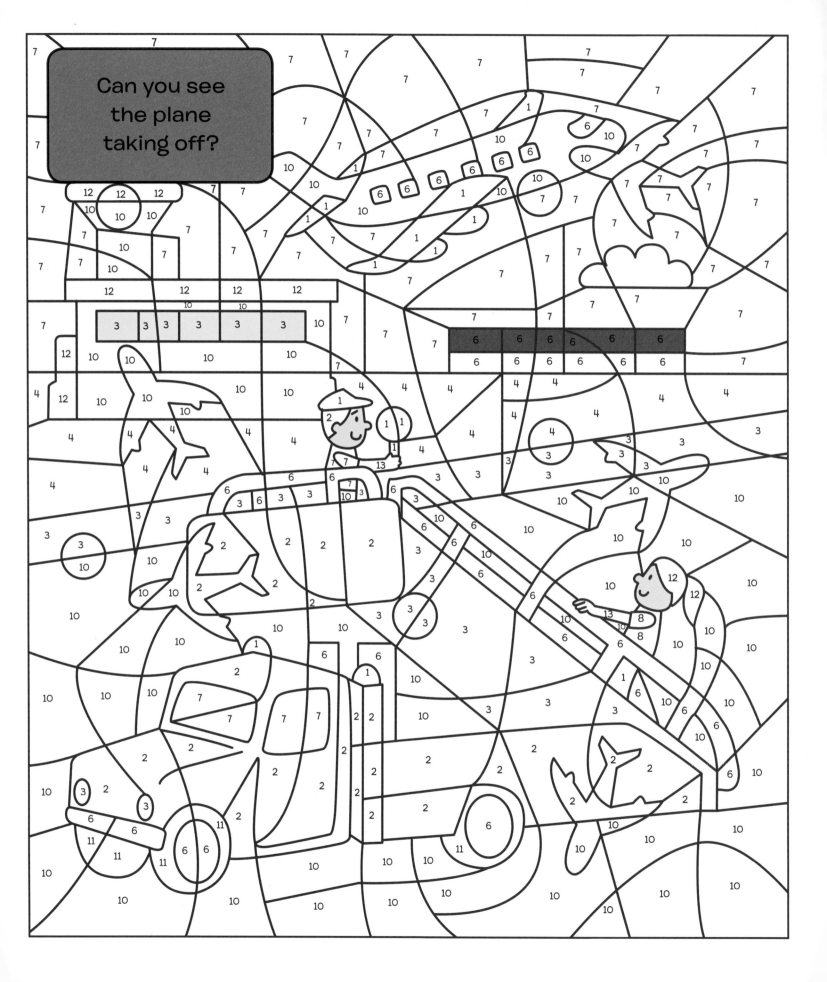

Can you see the plane taking off?

Let's take a taxi-ride in New York!

Amsterdam has very tall houses!

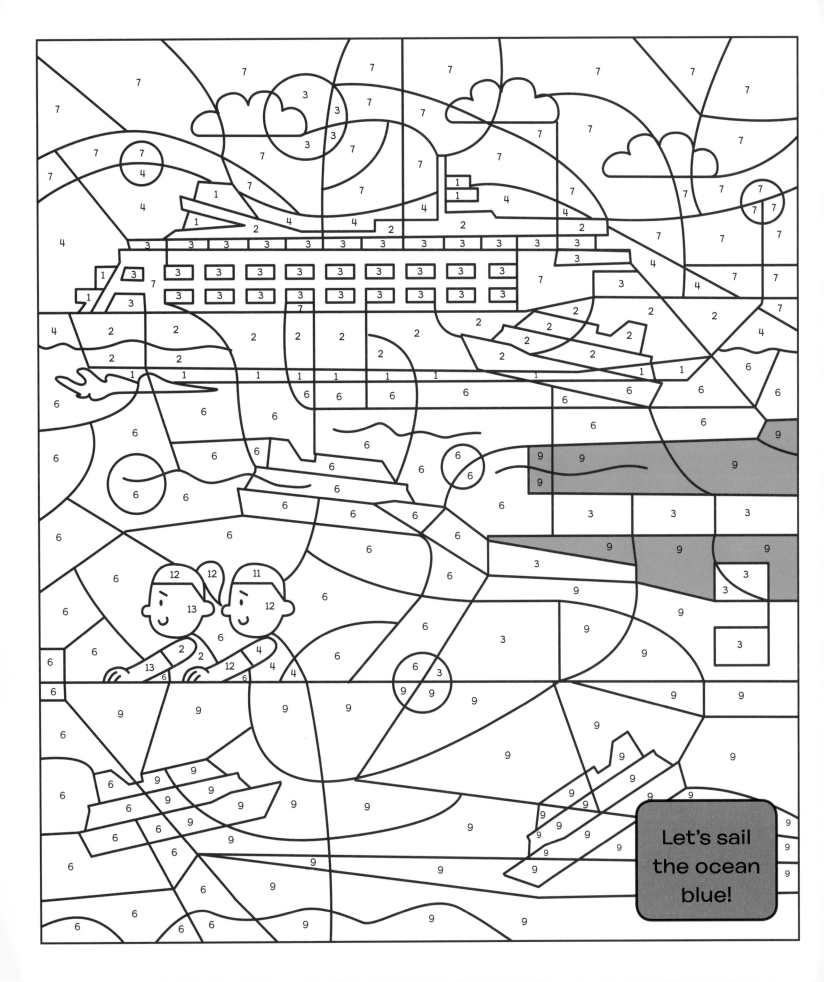

Let's sail the ocean blue!

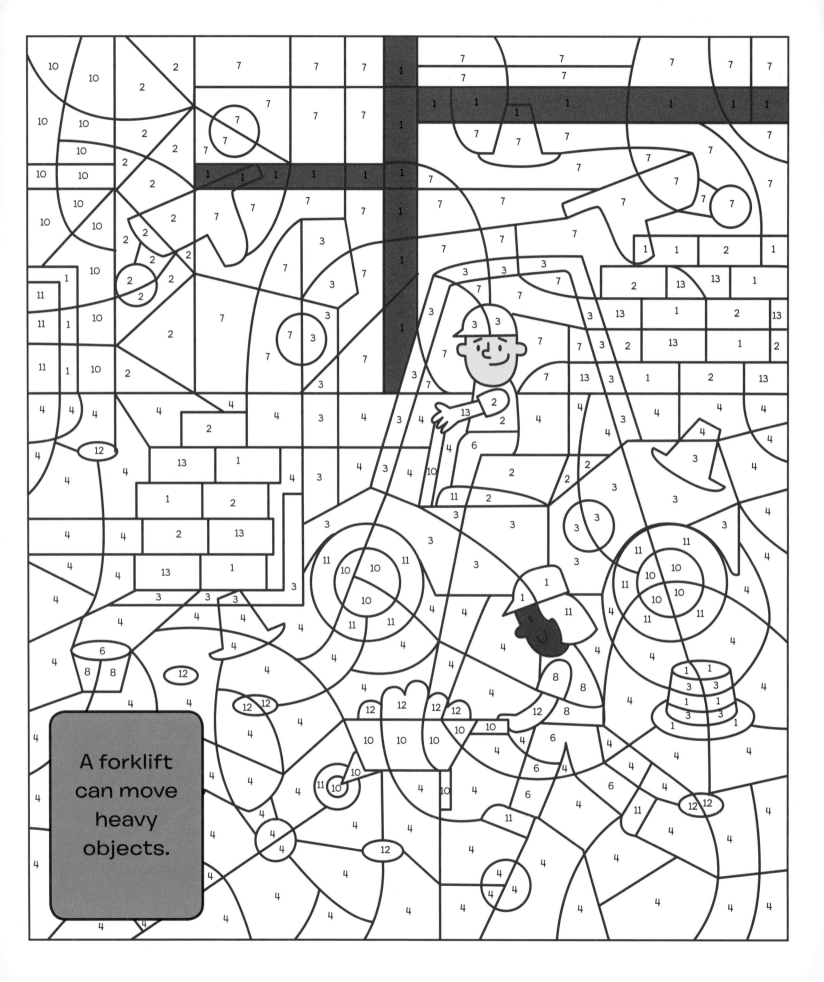

A forklift can move heavy objects.

A bulldozer can move earth and rubble.

What a cheery town this is!

Watch us jump these humps!

Strange lights in the sky, tonight!

Follow the arrow!

Let's dive to the bottom of the sea!

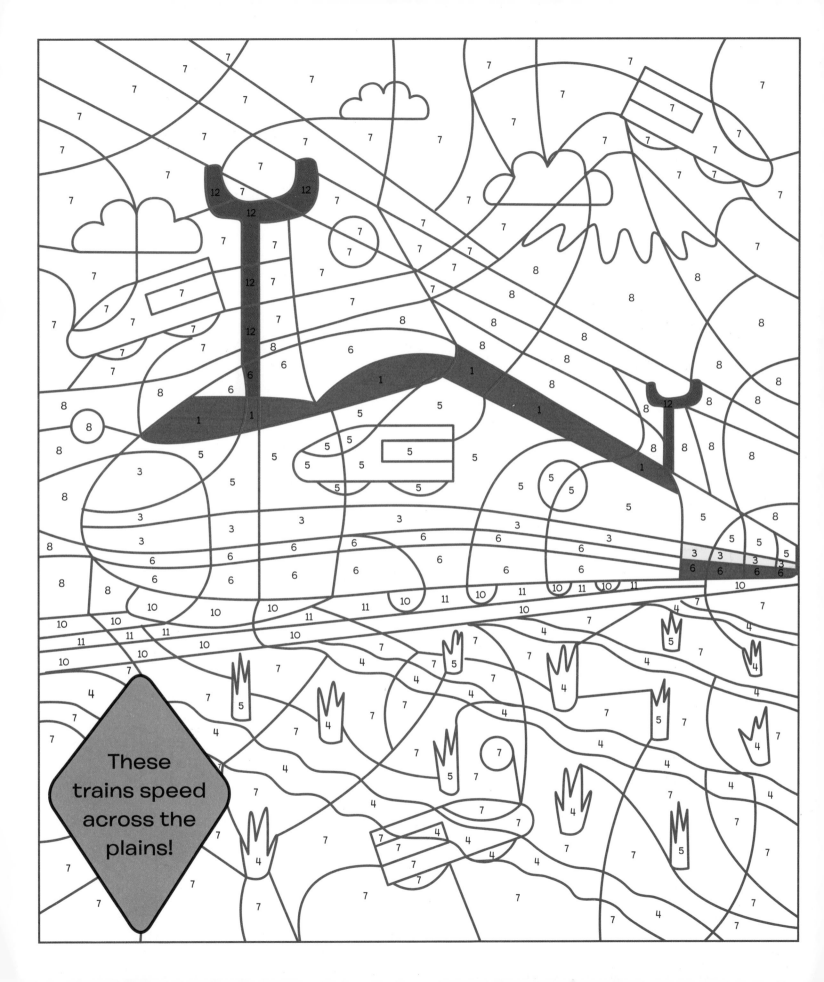

These trains speed across the plains!

This astronaut is out of this world!

These children are on their way to school.

Cranes are used to build tall structures.

These Vikings are ready to attack!

These Wild West cowboys are in wagons.

You need good balance to ride one of these!

The seagulls want some fish!

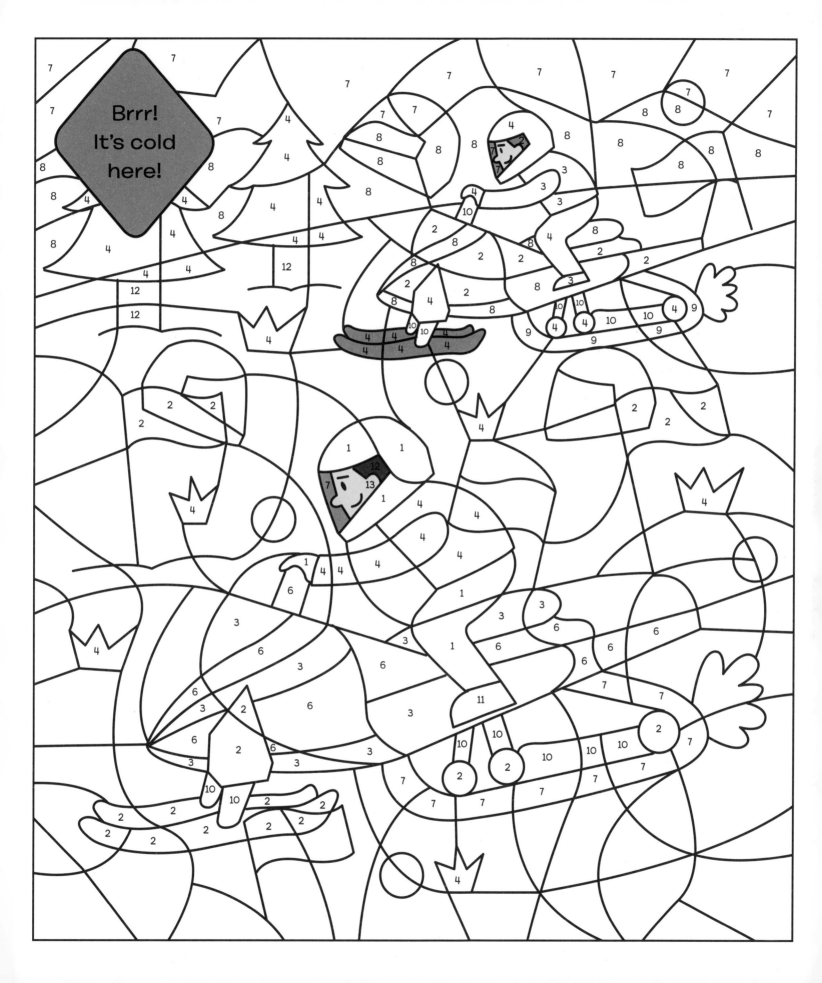

What a cool car ...

... and a cool motorcycle!

This vehicle makes the snow go!

This vehicle carries lots of cars!

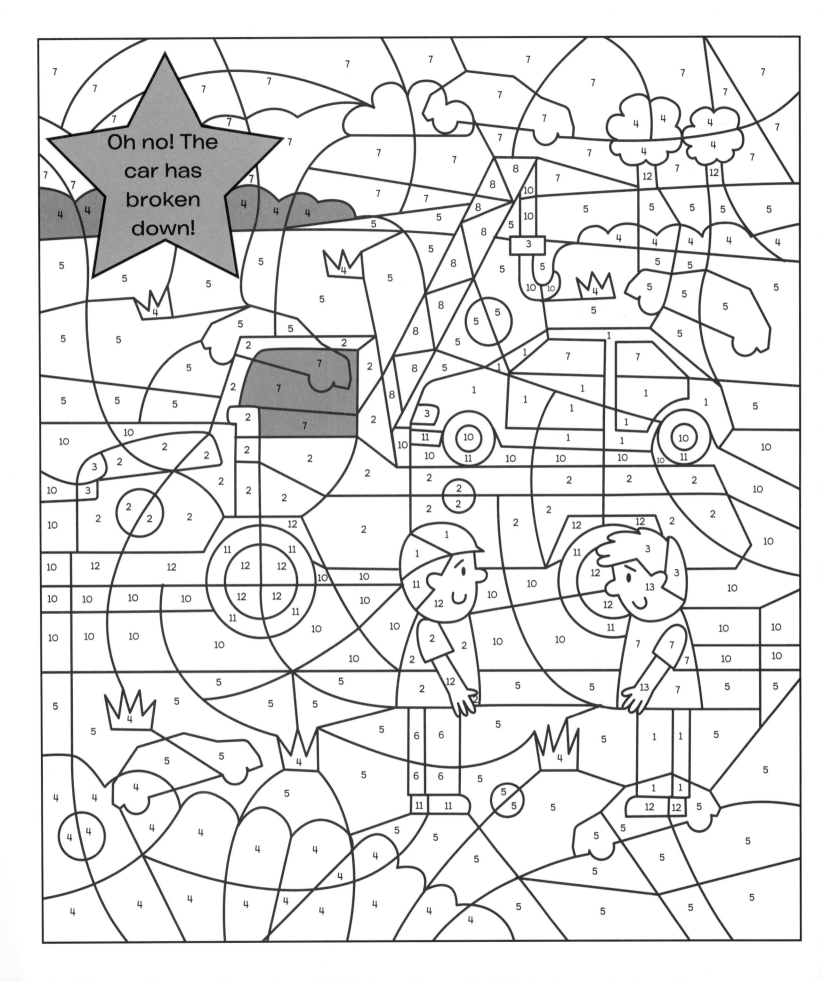

This truck has a huge engine and huge wheels!

This looks scary, but also fun!

Look at these fancy cars!

Let's drive across the desert!

Watch out for the truck!

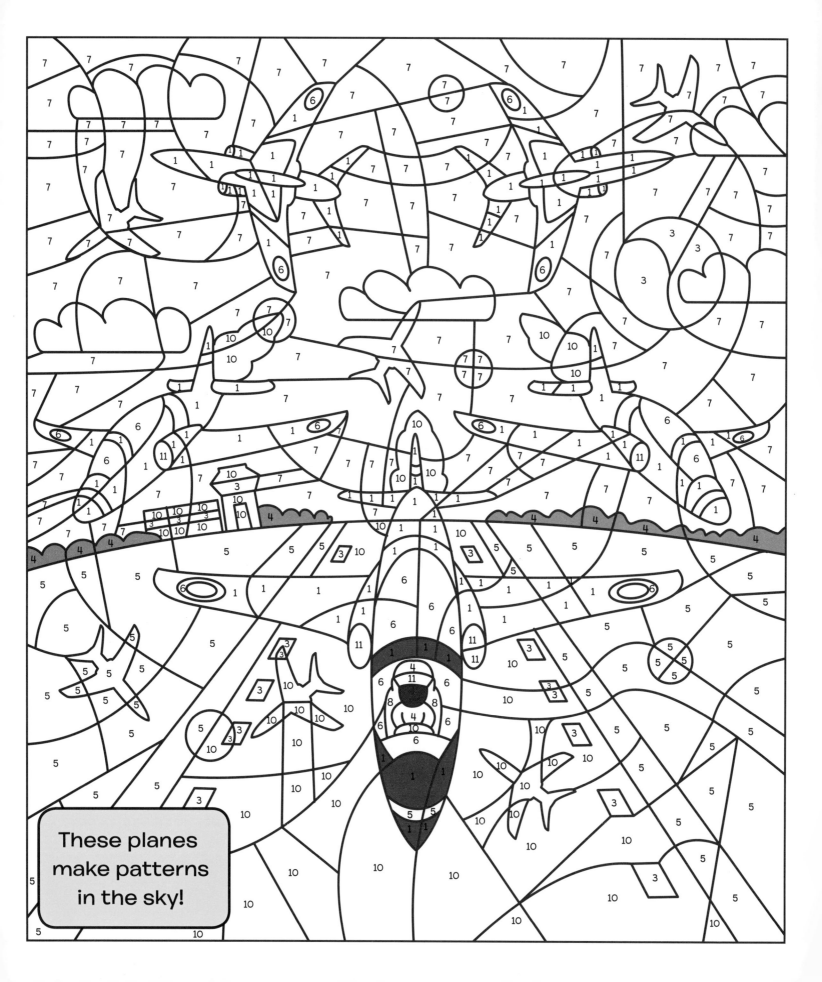

These planes make patterns in the sky!

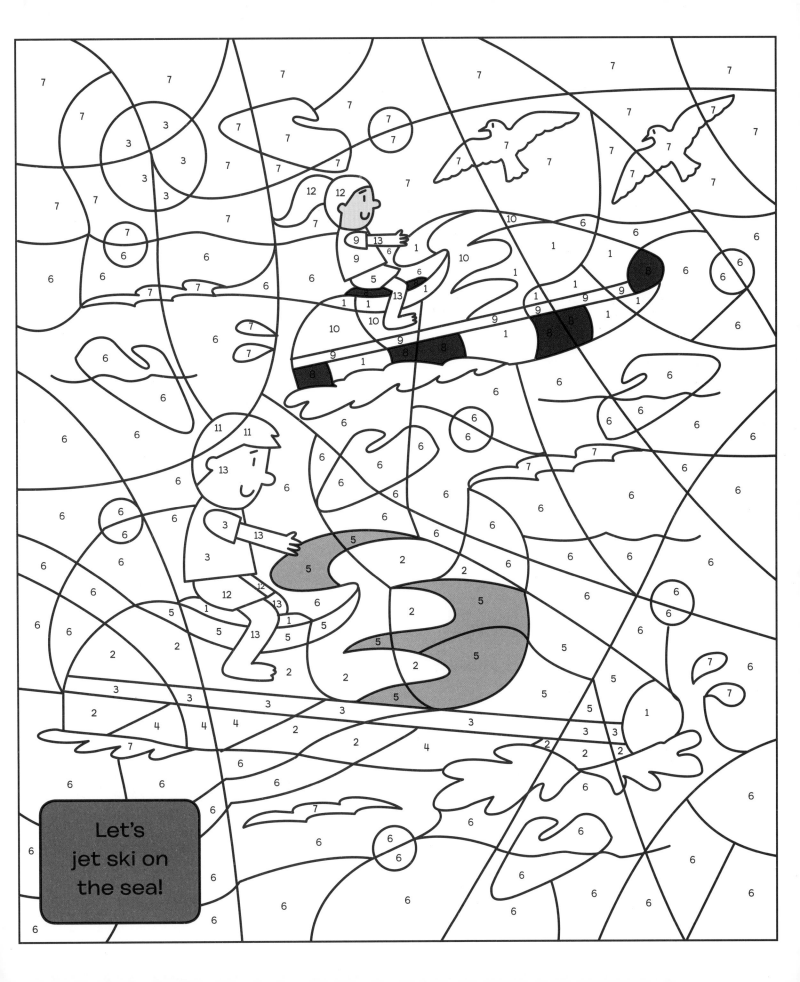

Let's jet ski on the sea!

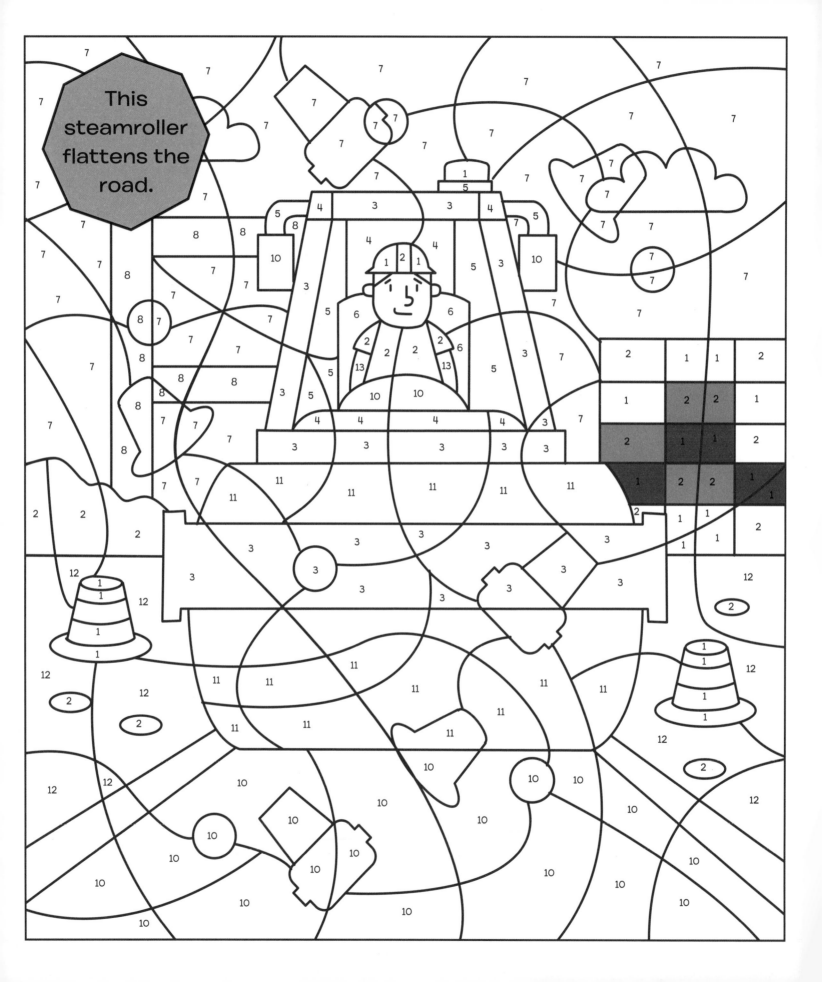

This steamroller flattens the road.

Venice is
a city of
canals.

Let's go for a ride in the countryside!

Pick vegetables with this harvester.

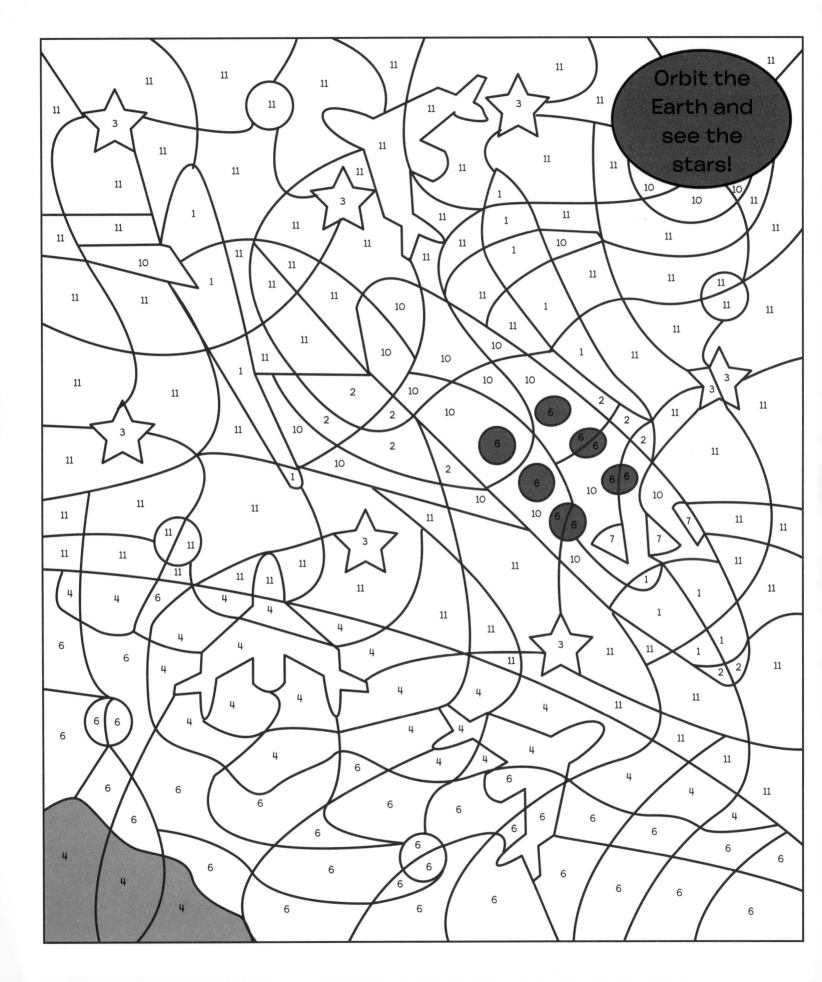

Orbit the Earth and see the stars!

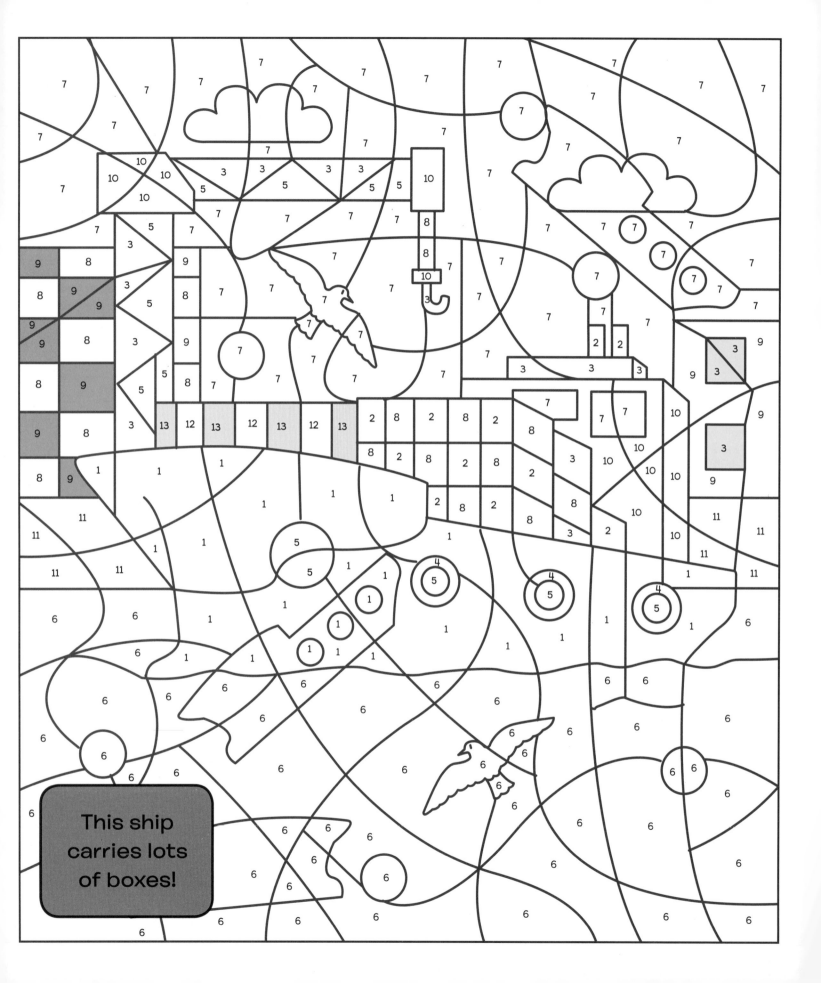

This ship carries lots of boxes!

So many trees!

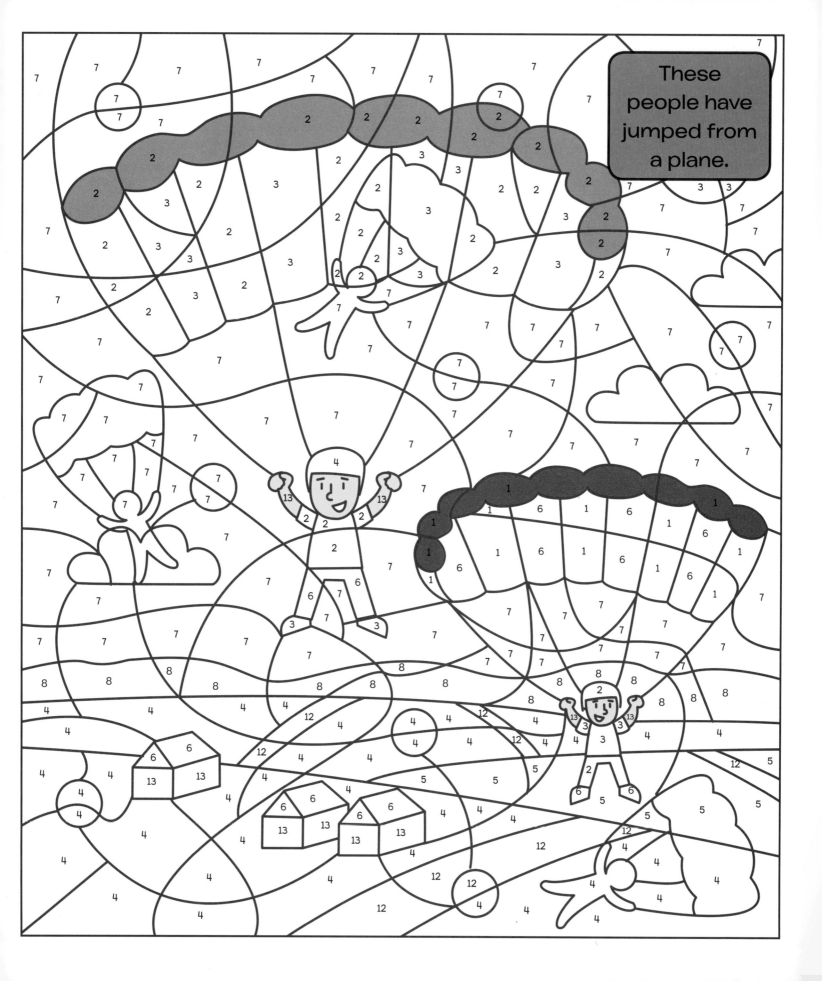

These people have jumped from a plane.

This vehicle knocks down buildings!

They're riding through the windy countryside.

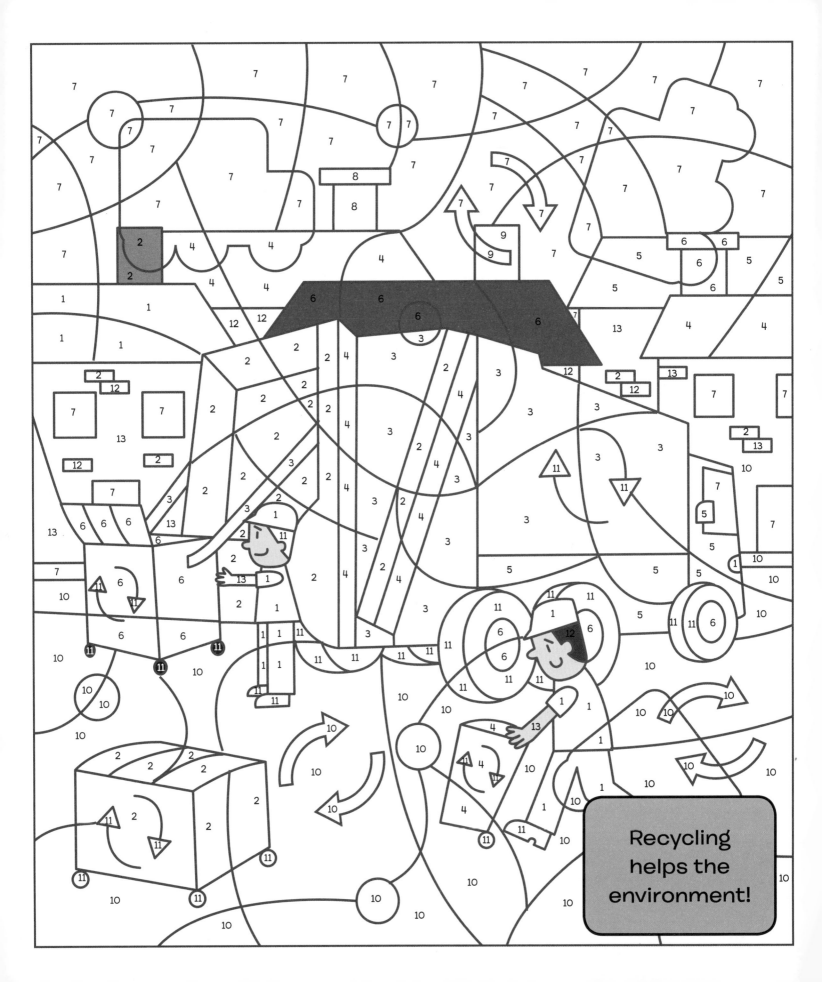

Recycling helps the environment!

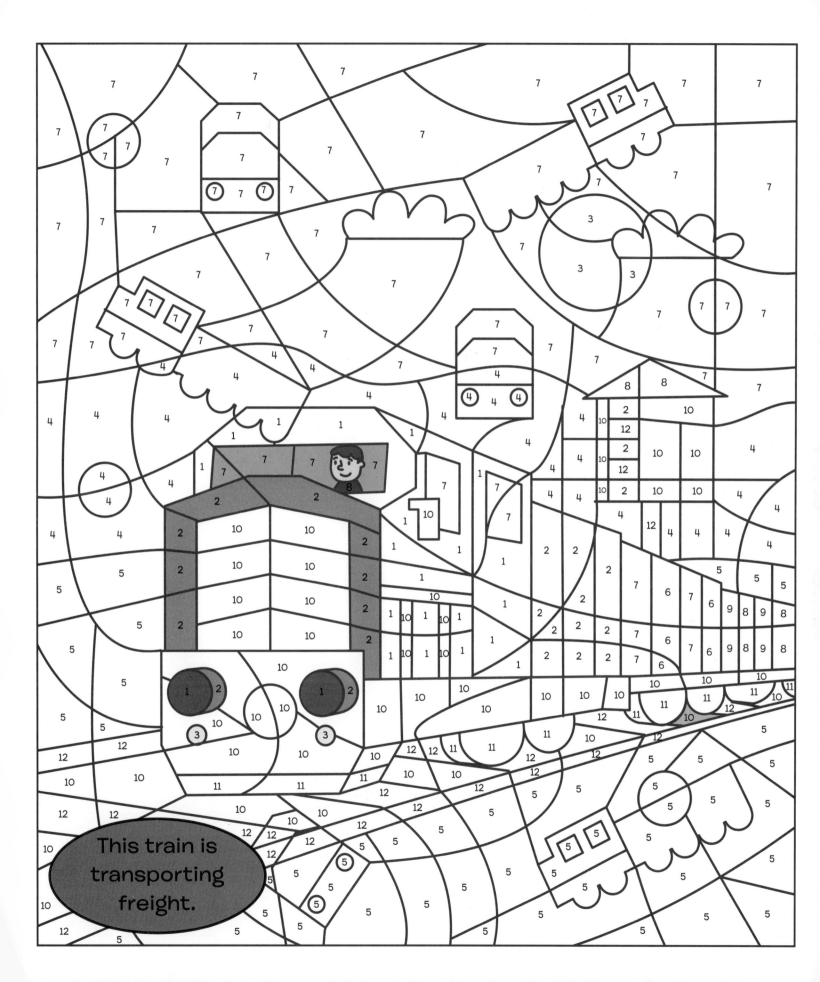

This train is transporting freight.

Pirate ship, ahoy!

A bus ride is a great way to see London!

Row, row, row, your boat ...

This scooter
is speedy!

Let's paddle across the lake!

This car runs on electricity!

This vehicle can drive on land and in the water!

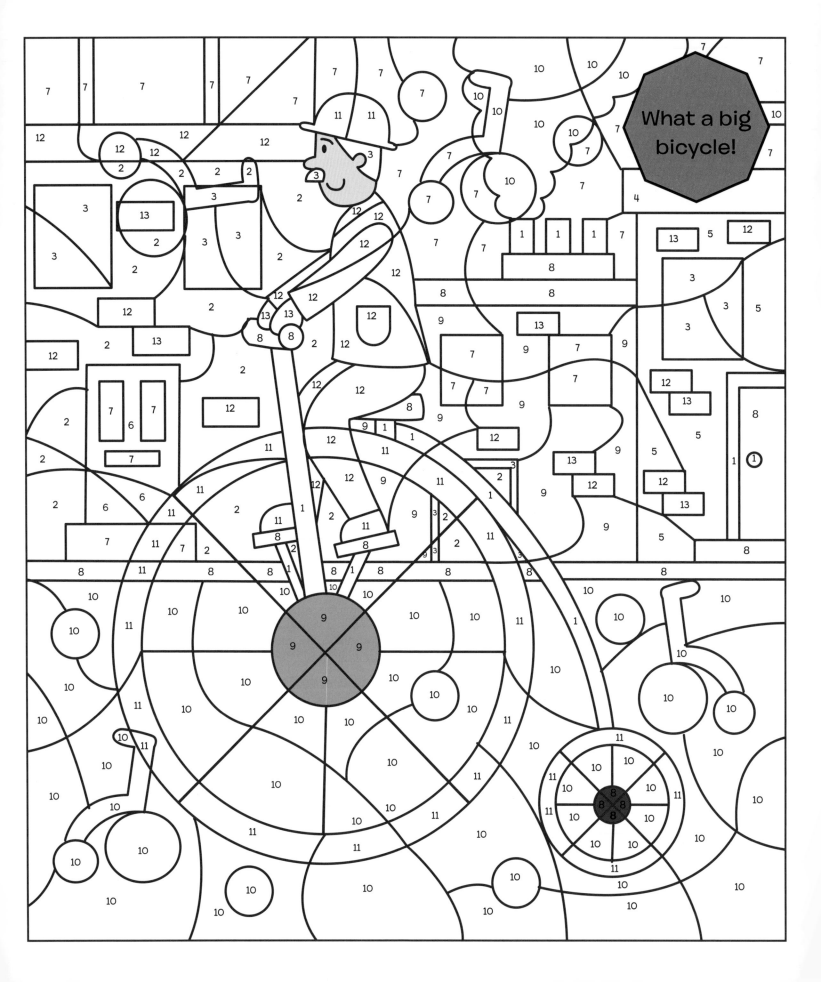

What a big bicycle!

Let's fix it!

This trailer is pulled by a horse.